MASHED POTATOES IN MY SALAD

MASHED POTATOES IN MY SALAD

An Alzheimer's Caregiver Memoir

Eunice L Sykes

In collaboration with

Barbara J Wood

Library of Congress Control Number:		2014915023
ISBN:	Hardcover	978-1-4990-6168-0
	Softcover	978-1-4990-6169-7
	eBook	978-1-4990-6170-3

This book was printed in the United States of America.

Library of Congress Cataloguing-in-Publication Data

Sykes, Eunice L
1. Alzheimer's. 2. Caregivers. 3. White privilege. 4. Interracial relationships. 5. Work place romances. 6. Racial lenses. 7. Government work.

Rev. date: 10/20/2014

To order additional copies of this book, contact:
Xlibris
1-888-795-4274
www.Xlibris.com
Orders@Xlibris.com
651272

CONTENTS

To all the amazingly strong women in our lives and to caregivers everywhere.

ACKNOWLEDGMENTS

I would like to thank family and friends everywhere who encouraged and supported the writing of this book, including my husband Don. Thanks also to those who completed early reads and offered explicit, frank, meaningful, and honest comments and suggestions. Your insights have resulted in a better book. You know who you are. Your "I am pleasantly surprised" and "I can't wait to see you in the bookstores signing books" feedback spurred me to press on; thanks from the bottom of my heart. God bless you real good! As always, may the Lord watch between me and you when we are absent, one from the other.

ELS

Thanks to my mom, grandma, daughter, sisters, other family members, and special friends who offered untold kindnesses over and over again throughout my lifetime. For, without your presence in my life, I would have been lost. God bless you all.

BJW

INTRODUCTION

No one can convince me that God doesn't have a plan for our lives. He surely does. I met Ramel Jackson at a golf league tournament in the spring of 2013. It was a pleasant seventy-five-degree day with little wind, blue skies, and white clouds in Georgia. We were cart partners for an eighteen-hole round of golf. Being in the same cart over four hours provides you the opportunity to really get to know each other even when there is very little conversation happening. Our chatter was in snippets as I have learned that, for me to stay focused and play decently and well, I must limit my talk between shots. Still, you get to know some of the nuances of the person you are riding with, along with the other twosome that are part of your group. That's one of the many benefits of golfing. In an unhurried environment among the lush and beautiful surroundings of nature, stuff is revealed, our covers are pulled back, and people share.

At first, our conversation was light.

"How long you been playing?"

"Where is home?"

"Been in Atlanta long?"

"What part of town do you live in?"

As we got to know each other, we talked about the game of golf. The pressures, being in competitive mode – rather than pleasure mode.

Laughter.

One of those interludes shed light on who she was and her life's journey.

I said, "Don, my husband, introduced me to the game of golf; we thoroughly enjoy our time together out here."

Remi, as she insisted I call here, mentioned lightly, "Bert and I enjoyed many years playing golf."

As I teed my ball, I could not see the green. It was about 450 yards in the distance. My target was the 150-yard marker.

I said, "My husband is starting to show signs of getting old . . . as we all are. Both of us are challenged with remembering where we left our keys and other things. He still beats me at golf though."

Light laughter.

"Bert died of Alzheimer's over a year ago."

Silence.

"I'm so sorry to hear that."

My second shot was straight down the fairway of the par 5, hole 7. I returned to the driver's side of the cart, covered my number 3 Callaway hybrid, got in the driver's seat, and headed toward our balls.

"From what I know, that's a dreaded disease. Did he suffer long?"

I pulled into the fairway twenty feet from her well-placed shot. By now, we could see that this hole was obviously a dogleg right, though we couldn't see the green yet. Remi was positioned near the ninety-degree angle. We could see water on the left and sand traps on the right. Something was across the fairway about 150 yards out, likely a ditch containing water.

She grabbed a fairway hybrid, number 4, I guessed, and sauntered to her second shot. It was aimed left of the middle but straight at the green, situated to the right and out of sight as this point. Great shot! Remi headed in the direction of her golf bag on the cart's passenger side, slid her club into the left rear slot, and plopped into her seat.

I hit the accelerator and headed to my ball. Remi chatted about losing a husband over the past year and a half to Alzheimer's. By now, I could see the green about 140 yards in the distance. I was closer to that stuff across the middle of the fairway. I had to decide whether I was going over the trouble or hitting up. I decided to hit up. I grabbed a short iron, number 9, refocused, took a deep breath, and wham! The ball went right, landed safely, but rolled into the tall, muddy, rough grass. WTH! Slightly disoriented, I stood there for two to three seconds, banged the club on the ground, gathered my wits, and returned to the cart thinking, "Not sure why I play this d--m game!"

Remi's voice brought me back to my current situation.

"My friend Jan and I jokingly talked about writing a book detailing our experiences. I met her at a long-term care home. Her husband also had Alzheimer's."

Had. The word stuck. I regrouped.

"I'm a writer. I'd love to do your story."

And so, here we are. Our goal is to "just tell the story," as noted historian John Hope Franklin once told me when I was writing an earlier book. Just telling the story means sharing the journey and the life lessons that came along the way. Those lessons are plentiful, they are meaningful, and they are well learned. They are here for you and for me.

I will always be grateful that Remi Jackson came into my life, serendipitously, if you will, on that special day at Acworth Hills Golf Course in April 2013. I am thankful for the game of golf, for without it, I would have never met Remi. She is a beautiful, lively, energetic, spiritual, no-nonsense, let's-get-it-done, down-to-earth way maker. She is a woman with a vision. She's a planner. She is a happy, positive, hardworking, thoughtful, fun-loving person. Her sense of humor serves her well. She has taken good care of herself spiritually, physically, emotionally, and mentally, and is positioned aptly for the rest of her life. Remi has sass and class to sustain herself. She has always listened to the beat of her own drummer and not to anyone else's tune.

Remi's grief started long before her husband's actual passing. Over 16 years she has dealt with situations, circumstances, and behaviors that slowly took her mate, the man she knew and loved, away from her. Her stages through the grief process – denial and isolation, anger, bargaining, depression, and acceptance – played out over several years and repeated themselves. Did I say Remi was smart? Along the way, she journaled many of her thoughts and prayers while going through, while in the moment. An unexpected resource, these notes were a big help and an unexpected blessing for writing this book.

Remi's spirit, her laughter, her frustrations, and without a doubt, her faith have kept her. She clings to hope; her sanity is in check. Remi is God's child. He holds her in the palm of his hand. This is her story told in her voice. Everyone has a story! Remi's is a refreshingly poignant, straightforward, positive, and uplifting memoir of dreams vigorously pursued and achieved, a career of promise, love, hope, and healing. It is an engrossing exploration of family, aging, and new beginnings, a story of friendship. Thank you, Remi, for your trust, your confidence, your openness, your clear and candid disclosure and for being my cart partner that day. This poem I wrote some years ago sums up Ramel Jackson.

Resilient

(From an earlier published work, *Instant Church: My Midlife Millennium Musings*)

Resilient is me –
A rubber ball
An elastic band
Stretch it
Bounce it
Bend it
Extend it
Snap it
Slap it . . .
God my soul to restore
He is the one who makes me soar!
Then I come back again for more –
That's me
Resilient is me

Eunice L Sykes

FOREWORD

While reflecting over my life, I have often wondered, "Where do I go from here?" This is the question I considered after the passing of my husband. One choice I considered was to allow life to take its course and see where it takes me. However, this is not my nature. I am a deliberate person, preferring to have some personal direction and meaning toward my next phase in life. My guess is that I do not want to miss out on anything by not ensuring I do all I desire to experience life.

Defining such, of course, takes thought, evaluation, planning, preparation, and execution. When I think about what I have accomplished on many levels, I get excited. Just the thought of what I want to do next exhilarates me with anticipation. I almost feel wild. I realize I have made many daring decisions resulting in a lot of hard work.

I have also played hard and loved hard. Would I change the decisions I have made thus far? Did I work too hard in my career? Did I love too deeply for too long or not enough? Was I a good parent? Do I choose to love again?

This book was in God's plan for me. Meeting Eunice Sykes on the golf course that day, riding together in a golf cart, sharing with her my thoughts of writing a book, and Eunice telling me she was a professional author and writer convinced me this was no coincidence. I knew at that moment that this was the beginning of a life-changing relationship.

After reading two of her previously published books, *From Kibler's Bridge to Miller Road: 65 Years of Christian Service in the African Methodist Episcopal Church* and *Instant Church: My Millennium Musings,* I agreed to meet with Eunice to discuss the process of telling my story my way. She made the collaborative process work well. She is very intelligent and patient and has been excellent to work with. She is an accomplished writer and is now a lifelong friend. Yes, God had a plan for us.

Barbara J Wood

CHAPTER 1

Detroit

One of my early vibrant remembrances as a young girl growing up on Detroit's west side was of my mom's sister, Aunt Lena, and her garden luncheon affair. I was about six years old and perfectly recited the poem "She Is Only Just a Rose" in front of Auntie's thirty friends and family members. Auntie gave me the poem weeks earlier. To be truthful, I had only memorized it the night before while sitting on the toilet seat! I had not asked for help preparing for it. Truth is, Madear – Mom – thought I was not going to recite it. That was the first inkling that I knew I was an independent, smart, fearless child and that I didn't need much prodding. Yep, that's me – Ramel Joann Jackson.

There I was, dressed in a pink frilly dress, with layers of crinoline slips underneath, hair neatly gathered into a ponytail, pink ribbon securing it, bangs tightly rolled to my scalp. In my small white-gloved hands, I tightly held a red rose. My shiny patent leather shoes and white socks with lace around the ankles completed my ensemble. Brave and unafraid, I recited that poem without missing a beat.

Once finished, I curtsied and walked off center stage. The ladies, mouths hanging open, clapped and cheered me on. Pretty good for a small six-year-old, huh? I've been driven all my life. I've never needed much coaxing, encouragement, or direction. Sassy I am!

Fast forward to the lively sixties. My coming of age years in the Midwest included rioting and racial conflicts not just in Detroit but in most areas of the country. Despite the climate, I witnessed a wonderful nurturing environment for music in Detroit, particularly soul music, that left a lasting legacy for our country and our world. Legendary music artists like Aretha Franklin, Gladys Knight, and Smoky Robinson were popular and their unique sound of Motown was widespread.

As a teenager, I often saw and met entertainers such as Marvin Gaye, Martha Reeves and the Vandellas, and Tammi Terrell. Stevie Wonder lived in my neighborhood. It was also during this time that Detroit, like the rest of the country, was reeling from the effects of an economic recession. The automobile and steel manufacturing industries were not experiencing hard times yet, though layoffs were starting to affect neighborhood families. Despite this, my childhood was normal. We shopped at J. L. Hudson's. We danced at 20 Grande. We socialized and roller-skated at the Arcadia Roller Rink to the sounds of Etta James's "At Last." We went to church on Sundays.

Motown was fast becoming the singing capital of the world as the Motown sound was generating enthusiasm and gaining momentum around the country. Our local sports teams, the Detroit Tigers, who won the baseball World Series, and the Detroit Lions in the National Football League were contenders in their conference. Our basketball team, the Detroit Pistons, was at their best.

Everyone assumed there would be plentiful jobs for them in the automobile industry. I never wanted that. I couldn't sing or play an instrument, so a music career was not one of my choices. What did I want to do? Would college be an option? Why wouldn't I want to stay? My sisters, my parents, and I have been here since I was born. Didn't I want to get a job in the automotive plant or one of their supporting industries? Those conversations played out over my young teenage years and still ring resonantly in my ears.

Contrary to natural inclinations, my daddy was not employed in the automotive industry or in any local businesses fundamental to car manufacturing. Rather, his work cleaning and pressing clothes provided for his family. Ever since I can remember, that's what he did. He was an entrepreneur, well entrenched in his dry-cleaning business. His work was relatively recession proof. He was a good provider taking good care of his family. Regardless of what was going on economically, people still needed to clean their clothes. His assistant, my mother, Madear, was at his side working the front end, handling the accounting duties. They met and fell in love at Arcadia skating rink, having migrated north from the south.

Ours was a Christian family with Christian values. Madear helped out frequently, though she spent a lot of time at home with the girls. Madear was a beautiful woman. Petite and small in stature, she was a brown-skinned beauty. Daddy called her Gypsy Woman. Her favorite pastimes included playing cards, the numbers, and going to the horse races.

My three younger sisters were determined to live out their lives in Detroit. Because I was the oldest, Faye, Ann, and Monique looked to me for role modeling and behaviors they should emulate. They all had their thoughts independent of mine on being in Detroit for most of their adult lives. I didn't. The oldest sibling has much more responsibility than those who follow. I helped my mother raise the other three. Yes, I didn't like that I had to be so responsible at such a young age. Indeed, I was upset having to be "sistamomma." I felt burdened and stifled. I had my own interests. There were things I wanted to do, like go outside and run the neighborhood. We could do that in the sixties. There was, however, one big advantage: as the oldest child of Ozell and James Jackson, I had a bedroom all to myself.

Daddy was part Native American, part African American descent. He came to Detroit from Birmingham, Alabama. Like many fathers in his day, he had a great work ethic, bringing his money home regularly and taking care of his family. He also showed few emotions to his children. He had limited skills to be a demonstrative, loving father. This too was not unusual for fathers of his generation. Most of them that I knew were unengaged with their children. Daddy was no different. It seemed to me that his dominant emotion, when he displayed one, was frustration – no, it was anger. And for me, it was not healthy. Daddy often showed anger toward me and my siblings – me mostly, as the oldest child. In some of those moments, when he was angry, he would jump on me physically and start punching me. Still, I would stand up to him. Not in an arrogant way but in a confident way that said I would not take it and did not want him near me. He knew it. Did I say I was bold?

My feelings for Daddy were not good ones. Our relationship was not the best. I kept a comfortable distance from him. I did not like him. I yearned for a better relationship, a better bond between me and the first major male in my life, but it did not happen. Like many fathers of that generation, Daddy showed few if any signs of outward affection toward me. He was emotionally unavailable. I mean, I got nothing – not a hug, not a kiss, not a pat on the back. Nothing! I longed for that. I looked for ways to assuage my unhealthy father-daughter relationship. And so, I immersed myself in school and in sports, participating in basketball, baseball, and swimming. I was a decent athlete and a good student.

As I matured into an independent, self-sufficient young woman, I realized that the need for love, attention, and affirmation from my father played out in many ways in my relationships with men. Over time, his lack of love toward me became issues in dealing with others. I so wanted a healthy, engaged relationship with my father. Those issues seldom went away. That was evident in my poor choices and risky male mates in the years to come.

I graduated from Cass Technical High School in 1964 and worked for an insurance company, then a manufacturing company. I eventually worked for General Motors but quickly realized I was getting nowhere fast. The jobs I had were basically clerical positions. One of them was at the Fisher Building, directly across the street from the Motown building (then called Hitsville USA), on West Grand Boulevard. I grew up among the likes of the Supremes, the Four Tops, and the Temptations. Since I couldn't carry a tune in a bucket, I subsequently enrolled in junior college. The Greystone Ballroom was lively all the time, with entertainers such as the Miracles, Supremes, and Mary Wells providing wonderful venues for entertainment. I enrolled at the University of Detroit. Though I didn't yet have any clue what I wanted to be or do as a productive adult, I did know that I wanted to be somewhere else, outside of Detroit. I was ambitious; I didn't know how to think any other way.

~~~~~~~~

My first love and my first lover was Jerry Stadem. Part of my attraction to him was that he represented a father figure to me – since to me, I had none or wanted a better one. Jerry was 6'1" and 150 pounds, and was ten years older than I when we met. He had served four years in the US military as a marine. He was very attractive – tall, dark, thin, handsome. He had street smarts. In fact, I met him in my neighborhood when I was 17. He was 27. It was a sunny afternoon. I was outside with a group of girlfriends. We were talking and laughing. When I glanced beyond my girl circle, there he was. He was sitting on a stoop. He had that swag, and I loved it. He smiled. I smiled back. He flirted, lifting his chin in my direction. I flirted back, cocking my head to the side. Wow! Here was an older guy paying me some attention. Thus began our relationship. He
~~~~~~~~

had his own place, an apartment, on the third floor in the back on Wyatt Street. He taught me many things about life: how to drink, how to smoke, how to inhale marijuana, and how to make love. To me, he represented a worldly view, one that I didn't quite know yet.

When we met, I was just starting college. While I was still figuring out who I was, my plan was to complete my education at the University of Detroit, get a degree, and leave the Midwest and leave Detroit. I was not sure where I was going, but I knew I was leaving Detroit. There was no doubt about that. Even when I suspected I was expecting, my made-up mind was unmoved. I was leaving first chance I got. Sure enough, at eighteen, less than a year after meeting Jerry, I became pregnant and I decided to keep my baby. I also decided to get married. In November following my high school graduation, I became Mrs. Jerry Stadem. Still athletic, my favorite pastime was roller-skating at Arcadia. Pregnant and roller-skating – what a sight! Dreams deferred, not defeated.

Our wedding was small. Madear had a reception for us at her home. All the family were there. I moved into his apartment. The place was smaller than our wedding and had little light streaming in from outside. It was a dimly lit place. A one-bedroom place situated on the back side of the street. Here I was, a newlywed. I knew we wouldn't live here long. Within months after baby girl Karen's birth on July 20, 1965, I found another place and put a note on Jerry's door that said, "We have moved." This new apartment was better, a two-bedroom unit, still on Wyatt Street, in the front of the building. Madear's mother, Grandma Niecie, took care of Karen when I returned to work.

As we settled into married life, I soon realized I had married an idea: white picket fence, three children, being happily in love. The whole kit and caboodle! I was focused, being a faithful, dutiful wife, building our corner of the world. I was temporarily satisfied. However, the longing to be someplace else persisted. Jerry, on the other hand, was hesitant about giving up his old life, his singlehood. I saw him around town in hotel lobbies. He was gone often. When he was not "out with the boys," coming home in the wee hours of the morning, he was bringing his friends around. Like Daddy, he worked and brought his meager earnings home. Even so, we fought often. He was physical. I was physical. I would stand on a chair and beat him. Once, I tossed a metal TV table at him when he entered the room and hit his head.

I was also dealing with post pregnancy hormone behaviors. I was volatile. Jerry brought out of the worst in me. I didn't like sex with him. I knew also that I did not want another child by him. We eventually moved again. Our third place was a house that we rented. Though I thought I loved him, our relationship soured. I grew tired and weary. I was not happy with him, with our life. After two years, I left him. However, I went back to him. Then a woman who rented the upstairs unit from us knocked on our door one evening, claiming to have some sort of relationship with my husband. I left him again, this time for good. This last incident confirmed what I already knew: he was not my class, not my life, not my man. I returned to my parents' home. Soon after, I filed the paperwork for a divorce. Madear, especially, did not want me to divorce Jerry. My guess is that she thought, "He's better than no husband at all," a mind-set similar to the way she had lived her life.

Life had to change. I continued doing clerical duties in a sales office. One coworker convinced me to go back to college and get a degree. She recognized something in me – drive! I did and graduated after two and a half years from the University of Detroit with a bachelor's in business administration and industrial relations. I knew what I wanted to do. I was looking for work in personnel, in a union environment. The best I could find was work in a manufacturing plant. I remained in the Detroit area for three more years. During that time, I purchased my first home. I was twenty-one. Karen and I lived in several homes, all of which were the typical Midwest type: Cape Cod designs, two or three stories, with small boxy rooms with even smaller windows, dark interior, and a basement. I learned to use mirrors on the walls to make my places look bigger, always waiting for the next best thing. I've always wanted a bigger, better, bolder, greater life, even with Karen on my hip. Though I wasn't sure what it was, I knew it was not in Detroit.

Karen was six when my sister Faye and I were invited by family friends to visit them in Los Angeles, California, for a week. Encouraged, we went. It was 1971. Once there, I fell in love with the lifestyle. I decided that California was the place to build my future. That visit turned my life toward the West Coast. People were strolling down the sidewalks, eating outside, drinking coffee at tables situated curbside. Hillside homes were everywhere; the atmosphere was different, cleaner (even with the smog) and brighter; and sunshine was everywhere.

This place was quite different from Detroit, where potholes in the winter were plentiful and people regularly partied in their basements. The relaxed, laid-back lifestyle in LA, with its amazing weather, beach life, surfing, biking, skateboarding, watching sunsets, coffee shops everywhere, sidewalk cafes, free spirits – all me.

Upon my return home, I formulated my plan and began working it. I immediately subscribed to the *LA Times* newspaper. I looked for jobs in the labor relations / human resources field. I wanted to be a boss. That I knew. It took four months to find the job. I looked for housing too. I wanted something in the Fox Hills area of LA. Never mind that I didn't know how I was going to pay to live there. In that particular area at that time, rent started at $450 for a one-bedroom place. I was currently paying $250 a month for three bedrooms in Detroit for a home I had recently purchased. The cost of living in California was a rude awakening for me. Still, I was determined.

I knew my decision to leave Detroit was the right one when, during my two-week resignation period, one of my supervisors, Mr. Frenchy, kissed me. He pushed his tongue deep into my mouth.

"I've been waiting a long time to do that," he said.

I hauled off and slapped him as hard as I could across his face.

"I've been waiting a long time to do that."

No doubt now that I was leaving. The lure of LA would not let me be. So with a degree and experience in hand, I returned to California in June, conducted a fast and furious job search in July, accepted a job offer in August, and negotiated a start date for September. Returning to Detroit, I rented my house and shipped my silver raggedy, noisy 1960 Buick Regal to LA so that I would have transportation when I got there. I've always been a brave soul. An older friend assisted me in moving my things. I purchased two one-way plane tickets for Karen and me, packed our belongings, and headed into the sunset. I never looked back. Failure was not an option. I was moving to the West Coast.

Lessons Learned:

> Ignore the naysayers. Don't allow anyone to shake your confidence.

You can do whatever you want in this life. If you dream it, you can do it.

Make a plan; set a goal. Do it! Make it happen!

Single parenthood should not deter you from achieving your goal. Give yourself time to regroup, then go at it again. Detours do not have to derail your dreams.

As much as possible, parents should allow each of their children to be a child; limit forcing responsibility on them based on what you need to do.

Parents should parent their children; they have an awesome responsibility and their influence is forever.

Encouragement works wonders.

Listen when people tell you something. There may be an insight or blessing just for you.

Find someone who has goals and aspirations similar to yours, someone special to share your goals, values, and spiritual beliefs. Do not be afraid to love, but be careful and mindful of the type of man you want in your life and your child's life.

Do not choose a mate to complete the "family lifestyle."

Do not settle for less than you deserve just because of life's hardships. Keep focused and persevere.

Set your goals, then work toward them. Do not jump from the skillet into the fire.

Do not be so anxious to leave home or a relationship without a solid plan.

A relationship cannot fulfill your emptiness. Fulfillment comes through you from God.

Your Lessons:

CHAPTER 2

Executive Director, Bi-Council of Interns and Residents

I negotiated this job title when I was interviewing for positions in LA. I wanted an important-sounding title and I got it. You've got to admit it sounds fancy, sounds important, sounds C-suite officer ranks, just beneath the chief operating officer. Truth is, it was highly responsible. I was executive director over 1200 physicians. When I started the week after I arrived in LA, I was absolutely overwhelmed. My work involved fieldwork; I did not have a company car. The job paid little. Many of the doctors under my watch had more than business on their minds. I remained focused. This was a major opportunity for Karen and me to leave Detroit, to move to Southern California, to taste freedom, to get on with my life, to pursue my dreams. It wasn't happening in Detroit. I needed to go. And we went. My long-term plan was to get another position within two years of relocating to LA, one that paid better and offered better benefits. My intent was to leverage this title in the future for a better opportunity.

After getting Karen settled in school and coordinating the furniture and car arrival, I spent my afternoons riding around the city, familiarizing myself with the highway system. Over the next two years, I focused on my career and on raising Karen. She was a beautiful child, obedient, playful, always making me laugh. At nine, she was developing into a young adolescent. Once settled, my routine was predictable: get up, have coffee, dress, turn on the news, wake Karen up, prepare her breakfast (she wouldn't eat unless I fixed it), see her off to the bus, then get in my car and head to work – or traffic, that is. Traffic issues are a part of everyday LA life.

California was all that I expected. I soon ran in circles that included fancy cars, designer clothes, beautiful places to live, jet-setting, increasing job responsibilities, great money, homes in fancy neighborhoods, rubbing shoulders with celebrities.

My kind of life. I loved it. It loved me back. Men – dating – took a backseat. I just didn't have time or take the time to date. Dating wasn't part of my "grand scheme," so it didn't get any of my time nor my attention. When I did date, it was an avenue to get into circles otherwise unavailable to me. Karen and work were all consuming. I loved it.

Eventually, I got a private sector job, working for Kamer Permanente, a major HMO. I was managing fourteen labor contracts. Karen and I were living in a two-floor townhome with two bedrooms. I was traveling all over the state, working with clients in the entertainment industry, education, gas and oil, electric, and health care businesses. I was gone most of the time. Karen stayed with my sister Monique, who had also moved in with us, when I worked late or was away. I was blessed to have Monique close by; we traded rent for babysitting services.

Because the world of mediation is often wrought with pitfalls, I developed a smooth flexibility to go with the flow. There are times when discussions go as planned. I can see the themes emerge while sitting in meetings even before all sides have presented their views. Other times, highly complex negotiations are fraught with great misgivings, diverse political agendas, and significant mistrust among the parties. Billions of dollars are at stake. I could not worry about my home life. I had to stay focused. My work impacts thousands of employees. I am good at what I do. People request my services due to my impeccable track record.

Lessons Learned:

> Many "no" responses often bring you closer to a "yes" response.
>
> Do not settle.
>
> Be determined to accomplish your goal; have a plan.
>
> I could not be derailed from the goals I set forth in my career. In my mind, there was no choice. I had Karen.
>
> Always do your very best. Something better will come.

Your Lessons:

CHAPTER 3

Wife Number Five

My life was rolling along in LA at a reasonably satisfactory pace. Karen and I were on a routine schedule that made sense to us. My sister Monique was living in her own place. After two years, I had moved on from that "executive director, Bi-Council of Interns and Residents" position to a labor relations role in the private sector working for Kamer Permanente, a major HMO. I was traveling in and around the city, less throughout the state and focusing on clients in the entertainment business. Karen was now attending high schools in the Brentwood suburb of LA. She wanted for nothing. Independent like her mother, Karen moved out when she was a senior and lived with a girlfriend.

The job was all consuming. Within a year, a commissioner (federal mediator) position beckoned me from the private sector to government. An industry colleague called to inform me of an opening. When I left Kamer, having met and made many lifelong friends, associates, and colleagues, my network was broad and wide. I was known and respected as a fierce but fair negotiator. I would stay in the government industry for the remainder of my career and beyond retirement.

Though I was dating regularly now, there were no serious suitors in my life. Men were not a priority. I enjoyed being single and unattached. Men who had all the toys (cars, boats, jewelry, drugs, and so forth) usually found me. I had fun, moving in and out of elite circles with ease. That is, until I met Duke Bonner in 1982. He was a union representative. As it turned out Duke, like Jerry Stadem, was older than me by eleven years.

That "daddy thang" continued to follow me. Even grown women hunger for love, attention, and affirmation from their fathers. By this time, my daddy had passed. Though we still had unresolved issues, I went to his funeral and felt little or nothing for a man who had birthed me. Under this emotional emptiness for a major man figure in my life, Duke and I became an item.

We were both attending a labor relations conference in the city. I had delivered a presentation on labor/management relations in one of the plenary sessions. Afterward, he made his way to me and introduced himself.

"Hi, wonderful perspective on the management side of the house. I am a union representative. I enjoyed your presentation. Name's Duke. Duke Bonner."

"Thank you, Duke," I replied, really looking at him. Seldom in these mediation circles do I see African Americans. He was definitely eye candy, fine as wine. He stood out among the many people in my view. This hunk was very tall, 6'3" and appeared to weigh about 225 pounds, with a Magic-Johnson-type build. Earlier, I noticed him across the cavernous ballroom networking among peers. His physical presence was definitely obvious. Again, he fit the major criteria that seemed to play out in my romantic life: tall, dark, and handsome and at least ten years older than I. My "daddy's girl" image. I was yet again attracted to an older man eleven years my senior. With Duke and the physical strength he represented, I saw myself being comforted, protected, loved, held warmly, being encouraged, and supported in all ways.

He was charming and clean; he smelled good. After a wonderful nine-month courtship, we married. I became his fifth wife. That turned out to be a mistake. Wife number five should have been my red light, but I ignored it. I loved what we represented. Things were great initially. Duke kept my life orderly, bringing me champagne in a bucket after long treks on the road, running my bath water, turning on the Jacuzzi. I was spoiled. Our love life was very physical. Extremely physical. Sex with Duke was different, more different than I had ever had. He was physically big. I mean in all aspects. This man had large hands, large feet, and – you guessed it – the biggest penis I had ever seen. Though frightful at first, I gradually relaxed in our lovemaking. It was often painful. I held back. I sometimes said no. Yet I, at 5'7", 145 pounds, soaking wet, feisty, and up for anything, felt sheltered, protected, comforted, and secure in his arms. I wanted that. I needed that. That the uncomfortable sex went along with him was something I had to do. Besides, wherever we went, we were eye candy to males and females alike.

Our life together was one of entertaining and socializing with highfalutin' folks. Though I was busy, life with Duke was not boring. Rather, it was a constant party. If I was working or otherwise unavailable to accompany him to social events, Duke went alone. His network included parties, women, alcohol, and drugs. I seldom participated, choosing instead to focus on work as a commissioner (federal mediator), my utmost priority. Duke was high or drunk much of the time. His eyes were glazed over most evening when I returned home from work. On one of those wild nights, Duke wrecked my hunter green CLS Mercedes, a prized possession. He was not hurt. My car was totaled. I was fed up with his irresponsible behavior.

As a commissioner, I was making fantastic money and traveling frequently, both in and out of town. I was well connected and gave it my all. Duke was clearly enjoying his status as "Ramel's husband." Eventually, he began feeling insecure and jealous of my success. He was hurt, embarrassed, and no longer confident. He felt betrayed. We began arguing.

It was 1984. A new position, district director, opened. Weeks after the position was posted, I had a telephone conversation with an industry colleague. He casually commented that I would be an excellent candidate.

"Hey, Ramel. Have you heard about the position opening in the LA area?"

"Not yet, tell me more." I lied.

"Seems a good fit for you . . . travel, overseeing mediation case loads, training, labor management negotiation skills, stake holders at all levels, superb decision-making skills. . . . Position title is district director. You would be good in that role."

I learned during the call that I would be one of several applying for the job. It was based out of Los Angeles, though the interviews were being conducted in San Francisco. That was typical. I relished the opportunity to return to the Bay area. I was still in love with California. By this time, Duke and I were in our second year of marriage. Though the home front was rocky, my career was flourishing.

When the bid sheets went up on the job board, I knew I was going to apply for that job even though I may have been underqualified. I didn't hesitate to throw my hat in the ring. My usual practice these days was to apply for anything that looked more challenging than my current position. The interview was not difficult. I interviewed successfully; however, I did not get the position. Like most of the upper-level management positions across the nation at that time, only old white men got these jobs. My new boss was Bert Adams. It would weeks, though, before I would meet him. I purposely kept my distance.

Lessons Learned:

Do all things well.

Do not be afraid to love, but be mindful of the type of man you ultimately want.

When choosing a mate or being chosen by a guy, stop and analyze why you are attracted to this type of man. Ask yourself "Is there a pattern?" For me, hell yeah, my daddy issues kept repeating themselves.

Professional networks are important to facilitate career progress. Don't underestimate them.

Your Lessons:

____

____

____

CHAPTER 4

The Kindest Man I Know

I was summoned to his office within three weeks of losing the job to him. My workload was heavy; I was traveling. I really didn't want to meet this man. After all, I had applied for the very same position, and he got the job. In any case, word on the street was that he was smart, demanding, and knowledgeable.

On that particular day, I was in the field working a mediation case. Dressed for war, I had on black two-inch Ferragamo heels and a brown tweed St. John's two-piece suit. My favorite lightweight cream-colored St. John's turtleneck lay snugly underneath to ward off the cool California breeze. Always fashion forward, I was impeccably dressed, never overdone, but quietly elegant instead. Today was no different.

I was on point, dressed to impress. This suit, like all my St. John's attire, traveled well. I never had to worry about having it pressed once I arrived at my destination. No time for that. The jacket, with the ¾-inch gold filigree buttons down the front and two smaller ½-inch gold buttons at each wrist area of the long narrow-sleeved arms, sat high on my neckline, where a gold 28-inch chain dangled gently between my perky breasts. The narrow skirt skimmed my size 10 hips and fell to just below my knees. I felt the same power surge I always felt in these settings. I was here to determine who won what and how much was to be paid. Yes, I felt powerful.

I arrived twenty minutes early as was my habit. In my world, if you are on time, you are late. The meeting room was long and wide. A deeply polished twelve-foot walnut-grained table was in the middle, surrounded by twenty-two fabric-covered chairs with arm rests. We were on the twenty-eighth floor of the Sidewinder Building, located in the heart of downtown Los Angeles. The view of the city was spectacular.

I placed my well-worn, elegant, yet durable soft pebbled black leather Coach briefcase on the table near the head seat, making sure the wide, adjustable shoulder strap was neatly tucked into the outside pocket and wasn't dangling off the edge. I no longer waited for someone to tell me where to sit. By this time, I sat where I could take in all the participants. How do you know where the front of the table is? It is where I place my belongings and take my seat. In attendance were representatives from all sides: union reps, lawyers, corporate management representatives, wounded party reps, a stenographer, and me, madam mediator. Over my twenty years in this field, I have come to know that these meetings follow a certain agenda. This one was no different.

Near the end of the meeting as we were wrapping up, I requested a copy of the transcript and the supporting documents pertinent to the case. The transcriptionist said he would FedEx them the next day. I gave him my card, said my good-byes, circulated the room quickly, and walked to the door. Down the hall to my right was a bank of elevators. I passed them by, heading for the nearest lobby phone. I dialed my office phone and checked my voice mail. There was one call. I did not recognize the phone number or the voice that crept from the earpiece. The voice was male, authoritative, and direct:

"Hello Mrs. Bonner. This is Bert Adams from the LA district office. I am the new district director for the southwest area. I am meeting with all my field personnel and still have to meet you. Please call this week and schedule an appointment. I'd love to meet with you and introduce myself. The number is 313-784-3008. I look forward to meeting you."

Click.

I quickly jotted the message on my notepad, returned to the elevators and pressed the down button. When the elevator door opened to the lobby level, I stepped out, signed out at the receptionist desk, and headed toward the front door. Turning left, I walked the two blocks to the Ninth Street Public Parking Garage. Today, I was lucky. My black 380SL Mercedes roadster (yes, I got another following Duke's crash) was parked on the first level. I could see it as I approached the entrance area. Over time, I had grown accustomed to parking several blocks away from the meeting site in order to give myself time to shift into work mode, deeply breathe, put on my gracious smile, walk tall and assured, and prepare to go to work.

Yes, my workload was heavy, but I relished every minute of it. This particular case involved a class action suit. My client list ranged from those in the entertainment, law, corporate, and medical fields. By now I had amassed a large client base, with referrals and callbacks. I was a top mediator in my vocation. I studied hard, read all the historical cases, and participated in workshops and conferences to keep my edge, to stay abreast of my work. I was passionate about all of it.

As I reached my car with keys in hand, I mentally surveyed the area, opened the door, threw my briefcase onto the front passenger seat, jumped in, and started the ignition. I backed out and headed toward the exit, turning right onto San Ledo Boulevard. I was famished and ready to eat. In this area of downtown LA, there are unlimited restaurant choices. I headed toward a favorite, Malonnie's. Within minutes, I entered the lot, pulled to the front, waited for the valet, got out, and entered the huge door. The crowd was light as it was close to 3:00 p.m. I ordered my favorite: a cup of hot lemon spice green tea and tropical salad with seared salmon on top. I then went to the restroom to refresh myself.

When I returned and settled in, the waiter brought my tea and water. I sipped the hot liquid from the cup. It was soothing to my throat and my soul. I reflected on that voice mail.

"Well. So this is the new guy," I spoke aloud to myself. "The person who got the job I applied for."

His previous role was that of federal mediator, just like mine. I didn't know much about him, though rumors were circulating. What I did know that he was white and was in his fifties. It had been three weeks since he began his new position. There were 31 of us working this district. It was a busy time. I called the number and made an appointment to meet him in two days.

~~~~~~~~

It was Friday. My appointment with Bert Adams was at 9:30 a.m. I dressed in my brown Ferragamo (these shoes are sooooooooo comfortable) two-and-a-half-inch heels. I wear the higher heel when I am meeting people for the first time. It's that height thing that gives me a sense of command. My suit of choice this morning was the tan St. John's three-piece pantsuit. I felt comfortable in my attire. I have always been a chic, stylishly dressed woman. I am thankful for my flair in clothing choices.

Bert's office was located near Brentwood. I knew the area. I had been to this office many times before. Traffic at 8:00 a.m. in LA can be highly congested. As I wove my way around the crowded parking lot on the freeway, I ended up on a back street and made my way to Colada Boulevard. The secretary, a Ms. Tomic, was at her post. I announced who I was and
~~~~~~~~

indicated I had an appointment with Mr. Adams. She smiled and motioned me through.

I walked into his office. He was standing behind his mahogany desk and waved me to be seated. Once we exchanged niceties, he chatted about my work and how he had heard many good things about me and asked about my goals. He said he could make things happen for me. I knew he could, but I wondered if he would. Time would tell. I surveyed the room quickly. A plaque with the name Dr. Bert Hans Adams hung over his matching credenza behind his desk. Since I didn't have my reading glasses on, I couldn't read the rest of it.

"Dr. what?" I was puzzled.

He continued, speaking of his plans for the district. I studied him. He was tall, maybe 6'1", about 235 pounds. He had neatly trimmed blond curly hair with sideburns. Those piercing blue eyes were captivating. He was a real hunk. He looked to be in his mid fifties.

"Only old white men get these jobs" echoed in my ears. I smirked at the irony.

He was clean shaven. He was handsome, very Paul Newmanesque if you will. I was taken by his good looks.

"What questions do you have for me?" He spoke with assurance and authority.

I snapped back to now.

Obviously, this man was well qualified to get this promotion, though I gave it my best shot. He wore a fitted, tailored navy blue suit. His silk floral paisley square was casually tossed into his chest pocket. Though I couldn't see his shoes, my guess was that they were well-shined Johnston & Murphy wingtips. His office was scantily decorated, yet there was an air of authority, such that worldly man items from Europe or the southwest would fit perfectly. It was absolutely a man's office, and he looked extremely comfortable in it.

I didn't answer on cue. I could see his hue deepening to an embarrassing red. He shifted uncomfortably in his black leather high-back swivel chair. I shifted awkwardly in my chair as I realized my hesitation caused a slightly embarrassing moment. My hard expression softened as the meeting drew to a close.

"Any questions, Mrs. Bonner?"

I cleared my throat. "No, not at this point. And please call me Ramel."

His formal countenance relaxed as he ended the meeting.

"Let's schedule a date for me to shadow you and meet your clients. Have Ms. Tomic book something over the next three weeks."

"Yes, I'll do that," I said, responding to his appeal.

"And welcome aboard."

I got up, gathered my belongings, and walked toward the door. Little did I know that my life was shifting into wonderful gear. Never in my wildest dreams could I have imagined the events that followed, the events that have brought me to this day, this place, this moment.

~~~~~~~~

Over the next two years, Bert and I worked on various and assorted projects. Our relationship was strictly business. I must admit this man was better suited to this position than I. As we settled into a routine, I vowed to learn all I could from Bert. He was respected and respectful. He was a dynamic trainer and mediator. I learned so much from him. He was polite. He was indeed the kindest man I knew. He trained me, he coached me, and he encouraged me. His ways were such that he was unafraid to share his knowledge, his resources, and his charm and charisma. He was a
~~~~~~~~

gentleman's gentleman, very polite. Once, when attending a large conference with over five hundred participants, we were seated at a table of ten. I went to the restroom. He was obviously looking out for me because he stood up so that I could see where he was seated on the other side of the huge convention hall and waited until I returned to my seat. When we were together in the evenings, he paid the bills, held my chair, and never raised his voice. He honored women.

I was learning from the best. I thought I knew a lot but I didn't. In time, my role became clear: Bert did the training, and I did the analysis, documentation, and reporting. He took me to workshops and meetings and introduced me to key people in the field. He encouraged me to learn the game of golf. We played together often. I was his backup when he needed another pair of hands. His total unselfishness and confidence in me turned me on. He was the teacher. I settled disputes and wrote the cases. I asked him to be a keynote speaker at a conference I was coordinating. He consented readily. He took me to his conferences and encouraged me to do presentations before thousands of professionals. He was not arrogant. To the contrary, he was very cool. We became close professionally. There was a yin yang symmetry at work for us.

Bert and I were a solid team in the mediation business. I had all the contacts and networks. My caseloads were across every sector. He loved my mind and my way around mediation. We complimented each other. Bert had the power base and influence. His dad had been a corporate vice president. He knew how to wheel and deal in senior management environments.

Bert's "white privilege" status opened up doors and access to opportunities for me that would normally pass me by. He was an extremely smart, highly intelligent, charismatic, savvy, and unselfish businessman. He was a wonderful mentor, sharing insights that made me better at what I did. Though his thinking patterns were different, unlike any I had ever dreamed of, I was never intimidated. Rather, I was amazed at how effortlessly he wielded his influence and power. He was fearless. I enjoyed learning from this man. Bert accommodated me. He taught me patience. He saw something in me and welcomed the role of mentor. He would say to me, "Ramel, you don't know how smart you are."

He was, indeed, a confidence builder. Everything he said he was going to do, he did. There were no limits with Bert. No racism or sexism to form barriers for him, to narrow his thinking, to invite hesitation, to lower his ceiling of expectations. Some of the evenings we spent together ended up in personal conversation and crossing-the-line talk. I didn't hesitate. It felt good and oh so right.

Though Bert was of English and German ancestry, I was not. It didn't matter to either of us. He taught me on another level what it meant to be powerful, to have limitless options. We had many conversations on handling clients, engaging the team, having all your tools, and working in a predominantly white male environment. We spent many evenings pouring over details relating to our work. He pushed me to do things I never even dreamed of. Like the time I spoke in front of thousands of labor relations professionals at an international conference. As I concluded my presentation and delivered my last lines – "I hope you have all the tools you now need to confidently win your cases" – I looked to my right three seats from the podium where Bert was sitting on the dais. He was beaming.

Later that evening, he told me, "I am so proud of you."

"You taught me all I know," I replied.

My heart fluttered; I felt like there was a baby growing in my belly. The cowboy from Texas and the city girl from Detroit were slowly becoming more than business teammates. Gradually, I learned that he was fifty-three (yes, ten years older than I), originally from Missouri and had three siblings. His mother was still living. He was married but separated from Mardy, his current wife. Their relationship had deteriorated to the point where she returned to Missouri. He loved fishing, boating, golfing, guns (although he did not hunt or kill animals), bucket hats, oversized belt buckles, boots, and all things cowboy.

Many evenings, both on the road and locally, ended in personal settings and intimate conversations between us. We comfortably eased into closeness, playfulness, and flirtatiousness. Often, the air around us was highly sexually charged. We were not physically intimate though. Not yet.

"Have you ever seen a black woman naked?"

"What do you think about dating a white man?"

"Why are you attracted to me?"

"But I work for you. How would that look?"

"What do you think about having a lover of another race, another culture?"

"Have you ever touched black breasts, black genitals?"

"What are people going to say?"

"We're an interracial couple; I work for you. This is highly complicated."

"Why don't black men speak to me when I am out with you – they speak to you?"

Queries like these led to feelings and actions that ended up, well, deeply personal. Once we crossed that line, there was no going back. Again, it felt right and wonderful, like that special dessert after a delicious meal. I enjoyed this playful sexual dance with Bert. Bert enjoyed it too. He was happy to spend time with me. And so, one evening, in a remote corner of a restaurant following dinner, he asked, "May I kiss you?"

I leaned in. "Please do."

At this point, I knew that I would eventually seduce this beautiful man. As if our working together so closely was not enough foreplay, I knew I wanted more. I worried, though, about the risks, my risks. I loved my work and did not want to jeopardize it. Even so, I knew he wanted more as well. I cannot tell you exactly when our fabulous working relationship became more than mere tantalizing words and longing glances. We had worked together nearly two years.

Honestly, I'm not quite sure what remark or action took us down this path. Perhaps it was the foot washing on the sandy beach in LA following our business meeting with the Chinese delegation. That moment happened so naturally. We were strolling along the beach, shoes in hand. As we approached the pier, he stopped, took my other hand, and turned in the direction of the water's edge. I followed. When the water met the sand, he stooped down, grabbed my right foot, and with cupped hands, he washed the sand from my right foot, placed my sandal on my foot, then repeated the process for my left foot. I was stunned.

It really didn't seem to matter that he was Caucasian and I an African American. Or that he was my boss and I his subordinate. Or that this was a professional relationship turned personal. Or that he was eleven years older than me (remember my daddy issues?). Or that he was a Republican and I was a Democrat. Or that he was a cowboy from Texas and I was a city girl from Detroit. Or that we were both married to other people. It just didn't matter. This multilayered, complex connection was on.

Perhaps it happened on a subsequent business trip to Las Vegas after, being the gentlemen he was, he escorted me to my room. I took a warm bath in the Jacuzzi tub and, still basking in the glow of a wonderful evening with him, called his room.

"Can you come by for a minute?"

"Sure."

Minutes later, when he knocked on my door, I opened it . . . in my birthday suit.

~~~~~~~~

After an exhausting evening of endless lovemaking, I mentioned my concern that our interracial relationship could damage – no, end – my career. Our pillow talk ended with Bert's absolute assurance.

"Do you know who I am?" he asked, gently kissing my forehead.

"I can make anything happen for you."

"Don't sweat it. Just love me."

I did. I loved him deeply. That evening in Las Vegas after drinks and the Dionne Warwick concert, we cemented our personal relationship. I recognized that Bert, the subject of my desires and love, is also my boss. He is white; I am black. I am a woman. I
~~~~~~~~

work for him. He is married. I am unhappily married. Bam! There it is. Wow! I am in love. I knew I had to keep us a secret. This was risky behavior. I knew that. I loved my career and wanted to keep moving up. At the same time, I wanted to learn more from this kind and powerful man. After all, he was the kindest man I knew.

Lessons Learned:

> White privilege is real.
>
> Mentor/mentee relationships are valuable.
>
> Loving a man of power is dangerous territory. Know what you are doing and what you are risking. These relationships are not for everyone.
>
> Bert's genuine quality of looking me in the eye endlessly and intensely during conversations told me that what I said was important. I had his full attention. I mattered. This trait made me feel like I was listened to and that I was important to him.

Career women must keep their spouses involved and engaged in their work life, especially when the spouse shows no interest for some reason (he may be intimidated). After all, successful people spend the majority of their time with coworkers.

When dating, do not limit yourself to a certain type, a certain demographic. Date people that you attract and to whom you are attracted.

With all odds against me, I picked Bert as a romantic partner. The other men in my life picked me. Bert was my choice, and ultimately, he was one of the best choices I have ever made. Even so, avoid workplace affairs when you are married. The reality is that people get hurt.

Follow your gut, your own intuitions. Disregard the other noises around you.

Your Lessons:

CHAPTER 5

Divorce Number Two

When I returned home from Vegas, I was not the same woman. I no longer wanted to be with Duke, my husband. Our relationship had already deteriorated. I no longer had sex or made love to him. Duke often remarked of my extended late hours, my constant travel, and Bert's being around me much of the time. Of course, Duke had every right to suspect a more-than-business relationship. Indeed, I was falling in love with Bert. I enjoyed our playful sexual dance. Bert enjoyed it too. He seemed happy to spend time with me. There were others who worked for him, but he spent more time, it seemed, with me.

Things were really spiraling out of control. After three years, I grew weary of Duke's irresponsible behavior. He was comatose the majority of the time, following me around the house – coked out. Cocaine was his drug of choice. His cooking utensils were strewn all over the house. At times, he would be naked when I got home, lying in the middle of the floor watching a sex tape and masturbating. He wanted me to stay home, get off the road, and get more involved in his party antics. I later found out that he had me followed and tapped my phones. I became more aloof. Actually, I was afraid of him. We were physically fighting. I was spending more time away from home and on the job. Tempers continued to flare up; he obtained a temporary restraining order. I got one as well. No man ever laid his hands on me and got away with it. My relationship with Daddy always prevented that. Daddy's girl issues were never far away. Actually, they were always on my mind.

After four years in this abusive relationship, I moved forward with the divorce, not knowing what my relationship with Bert was going to be, just knowing I needed to be free of Duke. Duke's suspicions frightened me. He had me followed. He hired a private detective. He confronted me and threatened to expose my affair. He said he had proof I was seeing Bert. Whether he was bluffing or not, Duke wanted a generous settlement to remain quiet. By now, I was making six figures. I consented to his demands.

As the primary wage earner, I needed to protect my future. That was my goal, to rightly divide the money and other assets we accumulated together. When we went to the bank to close our joint accounts, Duke's anger boiled over. Right there in the bank lobby. I am not sure what led to this fiasco. But before I knew it, our low-key argument ended up in a loud confrontation in front of several customers. He pushed me. I fell to the ground. Ferragamo shoes, St. John's suit, and I landed on the bank floor. I was devastated. My pride was destroyed. I began cussing and screaming at him. A bank officer moved closer and someone called 911. This catastrophe could have ended my career. I was livid. I was never alone in Duke's presence again. We were absolutely through. After the divorce, I never saw him again. I moved into a one-bedroom luxury apartment that Bert rented for me to the tune of $2,500 per week apartment. I took a month off to let things cool down, thanks to Bert's influence.

~~~~~~~~

By now, Karen was in her twenties, living her life, and involved in a serious relationship with a young man, Tony. She didn't have the same daddy issues her mother had, and I was happy she was happy. I shared my "Bert" plans with her. She already knew that Duke and I were having problems. I also told her I was dating Bert. It was a complicated conversation. I knew that I didn't want her to hear things that were not true. When I slowly informed my other family members, they were skeptical and warned me I was the one with the most to lose. Because Bert's family was out of town, living in the Midwest, their immediate reaction was a nonissue. They knew his work and his new love interest was keeping him busy. When Bert was happy, they were happy.

Bert and I continued our clandestine relationship another year or two before we became a public item. It was not difficult to maintain total professionalism since we were working separate field territories and had different cases. I was well known and respected in many circles as one of the best. My work record was excellent. Bert, to me, was like icing on an already delicious cake. I made him look good – better. He
~~~~~~~~

made sure I had assignments that showcased my many talents. When I looked good, he looked even better.

As time went on, our relationship became blurred with business and personal interactions. Eventually, we discussed interracial dating. It was more of a concern for me than it was for Bert. One event particularly stands out in my mind. At the Grand Ole Opry in Nashville, Tennessee, while making our way to our seats in the very front of the theater, I glanced across the audience and noticed there were no other African Americans in the room.

"I feel like a speck of pepper in the salt shaker."

"I hadn't noticed."

"You wouldn't."

On another level, we rarely attended events attended by a predominantly black crowd. Not a fundraiser, not a dance. He, in fact, had no sense of rhythm. He literally could not find the beat, even in making love. Work was our foreplay; we had sensual stimulation all the time. Our minds were in love with each other. We had stimulating work-related conversations all the time. We danced at home. I subscribed to *Essence* and *Ebony* magazines to stay connected to my people, to black folks. Though my world became more and more insular – there were few blacks in this field – I was always curious about the events happening to my people. It's true, though, that you can't miss what you can't measure. It was only when I moved to Georgia years later that I realized how much I missed black folks and the company of a black man.

I remained in the government sector for the balance of my full time career. And I would have a lasting, loving relationship with Dr. Bert Hans Adams along the way. The best ever! In fact, our relationship would last "till death do us part." And those daddy issues were finally put to rest. Bert fulfilled all my dreams and desires for a kind, loving, loyal, doting, consistent, enduring, mutually satisfying relationship.

Lessons Learned:

> Women, particularly black women, get over it. Your dating options are wide and varied. Take advantage of them. Don't be limited by someone's physical traits: black, white, Asian, Latino, or otherwise.

Relationships outside your race and culture and that involve the workplace, especially a superior-subordinate one, can be difficult and challenging. Only you can decide if it's worth the risk.

Go for relationships that teach you and bring out the best in you.

This relationship was not Duke's fault. I let "us" happen. I let him choose me because I wanted to belong to someone. I wanted a man in my life. I wanted to be safe. I settled. Don't settle!

You don't have to stay in any abusive relationship. Know that.

Some relationships serve as lessons for us; others will be blessings. Still others can be both. Recognize them for what they are and never, never regret knowing someone.

Your Lessons:

CHAPTER 6

In Sickness and in Health

It was 1994, our tenth year together. Bert was never sick. He worked tirelessly and was excited to be so involved. He lived to work and do what he loved. As district director of the southwestern states, his work was varied and his schedule flexible: He travelled extensively throughout Europe, China, and Canada, training executives one week, and in the nation's capital the next week, arbitrating. We were a great team. I had all the solid contacts and links to the networks in the entertainment and corporate worlds. We got extensive repeat business. Our caseloads were heavy. Bert had the wherewithal to get things done – the power base, the background, the title, C-suite colleague support, the budget, the charisma, the will. With him, I witnessed power like never before.

There wasn't anything that he could not do nor make happen. There were no limits.

On this particular day, I was working from my home office, tidying up several documents – my work now covered all field mediation west of the Mississippi. Bert was in town on a two-week break from travel, completing his paperwork, which was steadily mounting. He was living in the Southern California mountains with a two-hour commute to his office. Though he and Mardy were back together again, we considered ourselves an exclusive couple as well as professional colleagues (not to mention he actually *was* my boss). We lived separately, Bert with Mardy, I by myself. Yet Bert and I were always together and were very professional. I lived one hour from him along the route he took to go to his office. Most times when I worked in the field, Bert arranged his schedule to pick me up and accompany me to my caseload locations. This arrangement made it easy to move from our professional space to our personal space. He often spent evenings with me.

Looking back, there were no indicators, no clues, of any health challenges. I mean, Bert was in the best shape of his life. We were both extremely busy. Life was good. We were gloriously happy. I had no hints that our world would change so quickly and so drastically. It was daytime, midafternoon, when the phone rang. I was relaxing, sipping soothing hot green tea. Startled, I grabbed the nearest phone, the Panasonic handset, from its station. With the other hand, I switched the filtered water faucet handle to "on" and began filling a glass.

"Hi, honey."

"Hi. What's up?"

"I'm leaving home. I think I am having a heart attack."

His tone was very nonchalant. I was stunned into silence.

"Remi, I think I am having a heart attack."

Home alone, I was intermittently watching some news commentary on TV. I was unwinding after completing a long write-up of a recent case. I really wasn't looking at the TV; just listening occasionally for some tidbit that caught my attention. I can't tell you what the announcer looked like or what network was on.

"What?"

I dropped the glass. It shattered into a zillion pieces. Water was everywhere. Yet I could not move. I managed to sit down, trying desperately to gather my wits, seemingly scattered along with the glass shards. I grabbed my tea cup.

"I'm headed toward Grace Medical Center."

"What do you mean you're on your way to Grace Medical Hospital? Are you okay? What's going on?"

Words to that effect tumbled from my gaping mouth, like water flowing down Niagara Falls. I'm not sure which ones came first. It was as if another person took over my body.

"You should go to New Mercy Clinic." I didn't wait for his reply to any of my questions. "New Mercy is closer to you."

"No. I want to be at a hospital near you. I'm going to Grace Medical Center."

"I'll meet you there."

By this time, it was my heart that was leaping from my chest. I really didn't have time to debate. Bert was going to a hospital. Bert, my rock, was going to a hospital. He was having a heart attack. How did he know? Why would he say that? I could feel the tears welling up in my eyes. I took a deep breath, grabbed a paper towel, wiped my eyes, then quickly snatched my keys from the wooden key rack – my latest Tiffany trinket – mounted on the wall near the far end of the kitchen. I was so glad Grace Medical Center was only ten minutes away. It seemed like a lifetime. It was early afternoon. I glanced at my watch. It was exactly 3:15 p.m. Thank

God traffic was relatively light. I pulled into the emergency room parking lot on two wheels, parked the Mercedes in a space near the entrance door, turned the ignition off, took another deep breath, snatched my Louis Vuitton purse, and stepped out of the car and out of my version of normalcy. Like switching a light switch from "off" to "on."

Thus began my journey into my new normal. That's it! How quickly my life changed. It was really my new normal, part one. I just didn't know it.

~~~~~~~~

When I walked into his room, Mardy was already there, taking her wifely position on the left side of his bed. He had tubes and wires coming and going, like the spaghetti junction highway system converging in downtown Atlanta. I maneuvered around and over them, came as near as I could to his side, and leaned my face toward his. I wiped his sweaty brow. Yes, it was I who took care of Bert. I held his hand, asked what he needed, comforted him, told him I would take care of work matters, and assured him that all was well. Mardy remained aloof, taking it all in. Moments later, as I prepared to leave, she followed me out of the room.
~~~~~~~~

"I want to talk to you," she said in a curt, serious tone.

I turned and looked in the direction of her voice, not realizing she was behind me.

"I just want you to know that I really, really love my husband."

Steeling myself, I looked deeply into her blue-green eyes, pivoted, and walked toward the door. I knew she did not love Bert. She used Bert. He paid for her lifestyle. I refused to dignify her comment with a response.

Bert was transferred to New Mercy the following day. He had a coronary angioplasty procedure to correct the damage to his heart. When I visited him later that day, I closed his door, shielding the nurses' station some thirty feet away, gently moved aside the tubes and wires going in and out of his body, found his love link, and caressed it gently. He smiled broadly even in his uncomfortable state. He loved it. I knew he would.

"Be still, my love . . . let me love you."

~~~~~~~~

Bert returned to work after several weeks. During his recovery, he tried his best but was unable to keep
~~~~~~~~

up his workload. I did his job and mine. It was during this time that I was temporarily bumped up to his position of district director to cover his territory. At Bert's recommendation, I traveled to Texas to meet with the director to discuss and confirm this arrangement. It happened. Just like that. My responsibilities covered the southwest, including California, Nevada, Texas, New Mexico, Arizona, Hawaii, and Guam.

Within two months, my temporary appointment became permanent because Bert was promoted to deputy director of the agency, headquartered in Washington, DC. He transferred to Washington. Alone. Without me or Mardy. They were officially separated and eventually divorced.

I remained in LA. This situation lasted six months, the longest time we had ever been separated. It was a tough time. We missed each other. We talked nightly, both professionally and personally. Our love life suffered; erotic phone sex became our best friend. He was buoyed by that; I was delighted to provide us both some measure of relief. But I grew weary of the schedule. Actually, the time difference between LA and DC caught up with both of us. Bert had a second heart attack. My new normal, part two, began. I traveled to

DC to set up Bert's health care regimen, the best available. I coordinated his care with the medical staff at George Washington Hospital, handling all the details while still managing my district director duties for the southwestern states. The doctors put Bert on a clot buster pill.

That's two heart attacks, no major surgeries. I was happy. Bert was happy. But he needed care. My new normal was shifting again. I resigned my job in 1995 and moved to DC to be with Bert, to take care of him. No one could care for him like I could. I wanted to. I loved him. He was still the kindest man I knew. He was loyal to me; I was loyal to him. Loyalty has always been high on my list of virtues.

Between the first heart and second heart attacks – about two years – Bert's mother in Missouri died of Alzheimer's complications. I sent a floral spray as a memorial tribute to her. Mardy did not attend the funeral services. Bert really had to slow down; his workload was lessened. He decided he wanted to move closer to his family. He wanted to spend time with his siblings. We bought a house in Kansas City, Missouri, in 1996, remodeled it and flipped it. Oh, what fun we had! Throughout our relationship, we never argued. We disagreed on many things. But we never argued. Bert was not small-minded.

I was reinstated as a federal employee and worked the Missouri district. My extraordinary skills and experience were unmatched. Bert's recommendation made this happen. He always defended me. I had a sense of uncanny freedom because of him.

I met and got to know his family during this time. He had two brothers and a sister. They were militia types – armed, prepared citizens who provided for their own security and were insular, self-supportive, and independent. Though I was an outsider, they were kind to me. Jenifer, his baby sister, seemed to be his favorite. I remember when I first met her. Previously, we had many conversations by phone on his health, his work, and our move to the Midwest. She was pleased that he was happy, settled, and content. When she finally met me face to face, her mouth dropped, like some unknown malady had entered her being. Had it not been for those wonderful phone conversations and a warm connection already established around Bert and his health issues, she may have instantly ignored me, rejected me, and even hated me simply because of the color of my skin. Following Jenifer's lead, the others gradually warmed up to me.

When the Las Vegas office had a mediator vacancy in 1998, we left Missouri and headed west again. Bert was diagnosed with prostrate cancer soon after we moved to Northern California (near Oakland) in 1999. I was promoted to regional director. This illness was the third shift in yet another new normal.

After the bout with prostrate cancer, he asked for help. This time was different. Up until this time, Bert was a very responsible person, handling his varied duties and keeping the district moving. Now he could not train or teach. Nor could he arbitrate. He thought he could, but he could not. His body was showing wear and tear after three serious illnesses. We married in 2000 and within two years moved to Tulsa, Oklahoma.

The giant was looming. Our first sign that something else was going on occurred when Bert got in a cab to travel 300 miles for a class he was teaching at Michigan Central University. He forgot where he was going, so he took a cab on a 300 mile ride. I was still running the western region and was gone much of the time. However, after this incident, I promised myself that I would look into his health challenges.

~~~~~~~~

Though Bert had adult children of his own (from his first wife), he was not part of their lives, nor were
~~~~~~~~

they part of his. He wanted very much to experience family to its fullest. And so he chose to adopt my daughter, Karen, during this time. Karen's father, Jerry Stadem, had died ten years prior.

At dinner one evening, Bert thoughtfully spoke, "I want Karen and her children to have a father and grandfather figure in their lives." His totally unselfish nature astonished me. That same evening, Bert talked about moving to Georgia to be near my family. He also mentioned details of his end-of-life journey and began making preparations, including noting his desire to be cremated on a table napkin. I carefully folded the napkin and tucked it into my purse for safekeeping.

In 2006, we decided to come to Georgia. Actually, Bert and Karen schemed to get us here. Bert was sicker than I thought. We agreed he would request a buyout and full pension. He got both. Two regional directors retired at the same time, including me. We looked at several home communities, including a live-work-play community. Karen and Chip, my grandson, sent pictures of possible homes; they handled most of the details. We gladly moved. I was going to have family around me, something I hadn't had in over twenty years. My mom, sister Faye, Karen and her husband, Tony, and my lovely grandchildren, Chip, Colin, and Candi, were all in Georgia. Secretly, I was happy they were going to be around, even though we had regular visits over the years. Bert and I were older and had been through many ups and downs with his three illnesses and the demands of our jobs for the past 13 years. I was totally unaware, however, that over the next three years, the biggest caregiver roller coaster ride was still waiting to happen. My love, my strength, and my endurance were yet to be tested.

Bert's third heart attack occurred within a year after moving to Georgia in 2007. His fourth heart attack occurred in 2009. Again, there was yet another shift – make that two shifts – in my new normal, numbers four and five. His behavior was really strange during this time. For example, he was acting differently – making poor financial decisions, becoming short-tempered with people around him, and isolating himself from friends and family. Though the medicines helped his heart problems and no doubt saved Bert's life, those same medicines would prove damaging to other areas of his battered body. After numerous doctor visits and medical tests, Bert's diagnosis was clearly identified. We were devastated.

Lessons Learned:

After four heart attacks with a prostrate cancer bout in between, Bert's subsequent health issues seemingly escalated as a result of the anesthesia administered by health care professionals.

Current research points to a strong link between heart disease, strokes, and Alzheimer's. Know that!

Take copious notes in a journal to help you assess what is happening. As the major caregiver, do what is best for you and your loved one, especially if you are still working.

Caregiver's must be intentional about taking care of themselves as well as their loved ones. During Bert's illnesses, I was able to compartmentalize my life to keep balance and not stress continuously.

One very important detail that I kept was Bert's scribbled note on a napkin.

It was Bert's emphatic desire to be cremated upon his death.

Your Lessons:

CHAPTER 7

Alzheimer's

After numerous doctor visits and medical tests, Bert was diagnosed with vascular Alzheimer's. His cognitive impairment symptoms directly related to prior heart and blood vessel diseases. There were amyloid plaques and tangles in his brain. We were shocked. Finally, a name to put to this eccentric, weird, scary behavior. None of Bert's five previous illnesses, or what we had been through together, prepared me, his wife, lover, and caregiver, for what was next. I did the research. In a sense, Alzheimer's is a continually declining disease. Yet it is a roller coaster disease. Up and down, up and down, one day, fine, the next day, torture. You don't know what to expect.

You do know, however, to expect something. Bert's behavior was bizarre. I was becoming unraveled.

I took him to neurologists, cardiologists, as well as geriatricians, requesting test after test to validate what was wrong. What I learned was that there is an absolute link between heart attacks and Alzheimer's disease. Bert's brain was permanently damaged. The anesthesia that medical staff administered to save his life likely contributed to his cognitive decline. I was stunned. A caregiver's role early on, I learned, was to expect the unexpected, to go with the flow. This news threw me for a loop and left me unsettled.

For example, after we moved to Atlanta into the Sanctuary community, we eagerly reached out to our neighbors on the left, on the right, across the street, and behind the garage. Life was as busy or as laid-back as you wanted it to be. There were golf, tennis, swimming, walking paths, bridge, animal parks, fitness centers, and monthly scheduled activities galore. Bert and I embraced it all.

He began a daily routine of early morning coffee chats with several neighbors. On one occasion, Walter, a neighbor down the street, called and innocently remarked to me that Bert had been there for coffee three times that morning. After our chat, I was more deliberate in focusing on Bert's whereabouts.

It was after the fourth heart attack that Bert's memory symptoms became worse and more frequent. His bout with prostrate cancer made him weak, vulnerable, and less able to do his work, which he absolutely loved. I was worried, so worried, that I began that nervous laugh. You know, the one that comes forth when you really, really want to start balling. For instance, in public conversations, Bert would make things up. His comments made sense to other people. He was shrewd, he was smart, he was . . . Bert. I chuckled at these interchanges, thinking, "How witty is that?" But I was also thinking "something's not quite right here." I couldn't put my finger on it though.

Early on, his symptoms were sporadic, irregular, and vague. I ignored them. I laughed at them, thinking they would go away. Here's another example. He brought me coffee every morning, and progressively, there was less and less coffee in the cup. When I mentioned it, Bert returned to the kitchen, stayed there for minutes, then return to the bedroom, with the same amount of lukewarm (by this time) coffee in the cup. I looked at him, confused and sad.

He stopped ordering meals in restaurants when we went out to dine.

"Ramel will order for me. She knows what I like. Ramel takes care of me."

My nervous laughter again concealed what could have been and often was uncontrollable crying.

When I heard Bert's diagnosis – vascular Alzheimer's – I couldn't believe it. I was astonished. And yet I knew it was so. My beloved Bert was no longer the same person I fell in love with. I knew something was wrong. Yes, he had four heart attacks with a prostrate cancer diagnosis smacked in the middle. I worked and was his primary caregiver through it all. I was accustomed to his illnesses and taking care of him. I wanted to do that. After all, no one could do it better. My loyalty to him was undying. He bounced back each time, miraculously, though not as whole as before. This illness, though, was different. This one signaled an end, that part of the marriage vows that says "till death do us part."

With his Alzheimer's diagnosis, Bert's condition was a new experience every day. I slowly said good-bye to the man I fell in love with nearly twenty-five years ago and begrudgingly said hello to a dreadful disease: Alzheimer's. Bert was physically present in whatever state he was in, but psychologically, he was losing himself and I was losing him. Our relationship changed from wife-husband-partner to parent-child.

As his caregiver, I literally became part of his illness. By now, weariness was my most overwhelming emotion.

Bert began to wander in our neighborhood, getting confused and lost. Many times, he was unable to find our street. He would also wake up early in the morning and sit on the porch in his pajamas and robe, waiting for the morning paper.

"I can't sleep."

His calm state was eerily like a sea without a wave, when I discovered him there in the predawn hours.

Understanding and supporting the new Bert and his behavioral challenges were monumental tasks. Never once did I consider not doing them. There were seemingly infinite episodes. He took the door off the hinges, trying to open it. Numerous times he became disoriented in the house, though it was the smallest one we had ever had. He took candy out of a store without paying for it. He constantly fed both dogs, disregarding their scheduled feedings.

"The dogs are going to get fat."

"They are hungry."

Often, I laughed in the face of it all. This is an unbelievable illness. Wouldn't you laugh to keep from crying? Yet my heart ached.

An Alzheimer's diagnosis is a steady decline, much like a slippery slope with molasses on it. My new normal kept changing. I stopped counting. Someone had to be with him constantly. So my dear sister Faye stayed at my home with Bert while I traveled for consulting assignments. That didn't last long. After a while, I was afraid to leave him with the family. On one such trip, I taped a note on the guest bedroom door that said "Faye is here" so that Bert would remember.

I could no longer hold a conversation with Bert. He was often extremely loud. So loud, I assumed he had a hearing problem and purchased a hearing aid. He wouldn't wear it. He was argumentative; we never argued, though we often had different points of view. He slammed doors all day long, knocking pictures off the wall. When he punched a hole in the wall with his hand out of frustration, I knew it was time for additional help. I just knew. That punch could have been aimed at me.

Bert was a completely different person. He had always, *always*, been a gentleman's gentleman. He was the kindest man I knew. My loving husband was no longer the same. He had changed right before my eyes as if he were a chameleon in a forest, blending in wherever he went. Bert looked different. He was angry. He looked at me, blankly stared at me, in a peculiar way. I asked, "Why are you staring at me?"

"You are my wife. Because you are so beautiful."

I was scared, unnerved. Me, the brave, bold one. Clearly, I and my caregiver family members were at risk with his unsettling behavior. Though episodes were happening more frequently, I still thought I could handle and manage – no, take care of – Bert. My defining moment came, however, with the fist through the wall incident. He was so angry, agitated, and frustrated. Not at all like the Bert I fell in love with and knew for twenty-five years. "That could have been me," I noted, completely off guard. Additionally, he was not eating properly and had great difficulty talking. Frustration was becoming a common emotion for him.

On one occasion, Bert and I – we did everything together – spent a weekend with good friends, Tom and Cindi, in Biloxi, Mississippi. We were having dinner one evening and enjoying each other's conversation. I noticed Bert stirring his mashed potatoes into his garden salad. He then began eating this concoction. Our tablemates noticed also. Suddenly, I was sobbing. I couldn't stop. My nose was running profusely. I wasn't making any noise, but I was in full-blown tears, a meltdown. Bert looked at me and continued eating. Everyone else kept eating as well. Finally, I excused myself, went to the ladies' room, tidied up, returned to our table, and ended the evening.

I no longer knew who my husband was or was going to be on any given day, any given moment. Managing his medicines was an arduous process. Assuring he ate properly and on time became my next task. He was getting progressively worse. I was becoming more and more unglued.

Still, I thought, "No one can take care of Bert better than I," revisiting that notion time and time again. Never in my wildest lifetime dreams would I have imagined that I would be caregiving for a loved one with multiple, continuous illnesses over an extended period of time. He was sick for sixteen years.

Finally, after several months of going from home to home interviewing various management teams, I haltingly, prayerfully, and thoughtfully made my decision to place Bert in a home. After all that happened, my two years as a primary caregiver to an Alzheimer's patient – my beloved Bert – I was at the end of my rope. My sensible side knew this was the best decision.

In my search, I found the types of long-term homes available to be confusing: assisted living facilities, skilled nursing facilities (or full-time care), and nursing home/care home facilities were available. Also my biggest surprise was that the costs of care at various facilities were outrageous. I could not believe what I was hearing.

No, I did not have sufficient long-term care insurance. But I did have my negotiating skills. My years as a mediator would serve me well in researching long-term care facilities. By this time, I was studying all online resources. I wanted Bert to have intellectual stimulation. I wanted him to have male companionship. I wanted a place that provided these comforts.

After searching high and low, doing massive analysis, visiting several facilities, negotiating benefits and prices (because that's what I do), I felt ready to make the decision. Several homes were in the running. Two things drove my thinking during those difficult days:

Bert's behavior was continually deteriorating. I knew for certain I needed another option. The second factor, costs-versus-care comparisons, along with space availability, was my major criterion for selection. In all, Bert lived in three different places that accommodated his needs at the time. The Port at Vinings Place, an emeritus assisted living memory care community, near Smyrna, Georgia, started at $3,990 per month (plus expenses), was his first home away from home.

Meanwhile, there were never-ending ups and downs: Bert wrecked a truck. He was still getting lost on a more frequent basis. He became blind in one eye. He was frustrated. I was frustrated. Increasingly, we were in less and less husband and wife and more and more in child parent roles.

In my research, I became aware of respite care. One place that I visited was Methodist Village. I was intrigued by their arrangement where you could bring your loved one, leave them there for several hours (for a fee), then go about your business. I was invited to try it. The first time I left Bert I planned to grocery shop. Rather, I went home, sat on my porch, and stayed there for three, maybe four hours. The realization that I had not had a moment like this in I can't remember when hit me solidly and squarely in the face. Here I was, without anything to do. I didn't eat. I didn't drink. No wine, no food, just me. Nothing to get. Nothing to fix. Nothing to attend to. Nothing! I just sat there. I was invited to bring Bert again. And I did several times. While there on respite care, Bert played the piano and sang (he had a great voice) to the people living there. They were delighted. It was a win-win solution.

As an Alzheimer's caregiver, questions constantly came up: Who do you trust? Your loved one with Alzheimer's or someone else? Or something else? How much do you trust? I found in time that, instead of saying the collaborative "Let's think about it," the response was an outright "no." I lacked sleep and was extremely tired. My emotions were always in turmoil and ran the gamut: relieved and crushed, guilt, unnerved, worn thin, livid, suspicious, physically going behind him, in front of him, beside him. In Bert's mind, Dr. Adams, the industrial psychologist, became Dr. Adams, the physician. That was his reality. He acted like a physician at the nursing home and got in trouble for it.

I met Sheba at The Port facility. Her husband, Larry, was an Alzheimer's patient there. At 6'4", Larry stood apart from the rest of the patients. He and Bert became good friends. Sheba and I connected and became dear friends. Another friend I met on this journey was Jan, whose husband, Lee, was an Alzheimer's patient at one of the facilities. Jan, Sheba, and I became dear friends, leaning on and supporting each other during extremely difficult times.

~~~~~~~~

Bert was at The Port facility when he was accused having sex with a female patient. Actually, he didn't have sex with her. The staff discovered them in bed together. I remember when the management team called. It was on a Monday morning.

"Good morning, Mrs. Adams. Can you come to the home sometime this morning?"

When I got there, I had my smile plastered across my face, anxious to hear the latest episode.

"We found Bert in bed this morning with Ms. Janet"

"Well, he needs love and caring. I am glad he found it," I said, knowing that often he would not even go to bed. Or that the staff sometimes tied him to the bed.

~~~~~~~~

It was now winter of 2010, and Bert's continued agitation manifested itself in him being up all night, peeing in two rooms, walking around naked, and bed-wetting. To soothe everyone, I brought the dogs Jazzy and Billy Boy with me to entertain residents. They seemed to enjoy their company. I spent numerous candlelight vigils at the home, often arriving to find Bert asleep in a chair. Many times, I lost it and cried. After my pity party, I exercised both of his legs, shaved his face, washed his hair, and hugged and kissed him. That was my routine.

While at Clinton House in Snellville, Bert fell out of his bed and broke his hip and his femur. Earlier, one of the directors suggested I buy Bert a bed with a rail. However, before I could do that, he rolled over and out of the bed onto the floor.

After his fall, Bert required physical therapy. I moved him to Methodist Cottage ($5,500 per month plus expenses, like grooming supplies, linen, medications, and toiletries) for rehabilitation therapy. He was there three months. Little did I know that this would be his final care facility. Bert, my kind, gentle, strong, loving, considerate, loyal, smart, honorable husband, who was a great grandfather, a giant among men, was dying an undignified death. It was my honor, though, to be his life partner and to remain at his side.

Lessons Learned:

> Frequently, despite their best efforts, people end up with mashed potatoes

in their salad. So what? Is it good? It's certainly different. Does that make it bad? Not necessarily. Deciding how to respond is the ultimate goal. Will the response be humor, acceptance, anger, resistance? Will we become annoyed or out-and-out livid at best? Will we instead stay calm, pleasant, and light hearted? The mashed potatoes in my salad metaphor hit me squarely in the face, crises after crises. To diffuse road rage, I decided to recover and regroup, dust myself off, take a deep breath, and move on.

Heart attack and Alzheimer's links are real and strong.

As a primary caregiver, others do not see what you see nor experience what you experience. Often, the patient's family will insist you do what is best for their loved one. Your family will tell you to do what is best for you. The truth is, you, your research, and your faith are your best decision-making tools.

Respite care is a blessing. Use it as often as you can.

Cost of care can be negotiable. Ask, offer, inquire, barter, suggest, research, and do all you can to arm yourself with information. Remember, too, that cheaper is not always better. Loss of time and energy takes its toll on you, the caregiver, as well.

Before any diagnosis, purchase long-term care insurance even before you need it or anticipate needing it. Yes, it is expensive, often prohibitive. Still, it is relatively cheap when compared to the cost of reasonable long term care, anywhere from $3,000–$5,000 per month.

Discuss the best options for your financial situation. There are ways to get insurance coverage, for a rehabilitation stay, for example, that are not available otherwise.

Order your affairs early. Complete the paperwork for health directives, advanced directives, health care proxies, and/or financial directives while your loved one is able to make their wishes known. Remember that note Bert wrote regarding cremation that I tucked into my purse? It was crucial in the years to come.

Guilt is a real emotion during difficult times. Immediately after your visits, plan to do something to occupy your mind.

For your sanity, do not select a long-term care facility too close to where you live; it will lessen your temptation to visit too often.

Join a support group for Alzheimer's patients and caregivers. There are ample resources; pick those suitable for you and your journey.

Make use of the excellent online resources, like momsplace.org and alz.org.

Consult with various health care providers, including geriatricians, on your loved one's diagnosis. Ask them to run tests to determine or validate what you have already heard.

Caregivers, especially Alzheimer's caregivers, must be diligent about their own health and self-care. Get annual physicals with appropriate follow-ups. Don't forget dental visits and cleanings regularly. Exercise frequently. Schedule a massage once a month. Be intentional about scheduling "me" time.

Keep a journal as often as you can. Your raw emotions experienced "in the moment" will provide powerful insights and validation for your decisions later because you will second-guess yourself. Your notes will remind you of how far you've come and of your inner strength and resilience.

Your Lessons:

CHAPTER 8

Until Death Do Us Part: The Celebration

My telephone rang at 8:30 p.m. on Friday evening. It was New Year's Eve 2010. I was preparing food in my kitchen for a small New Year's celebration at our home. The cutting board was full of chopped onions, green peppers, and celery waiting to be added to the cooling cubed potatoes sitting in the crystal bowl on the counter. Family was milling around. I was headed to the refrigerator to get the salad dressing. I grabbed the phone sitting on the breakfast bar.

"Bert stopped breathing!"

It was Nona, a supervisor at Methodist Cottage. I started sobbing. Uncontrollably. My sister Faye, my daughter, Karen, her husband, Tony, and my three grandbabies were at home with me.

"Bert is being transported to Hobb Hospital. . . . You should go there."

I gathered my things, along with Bert's health care directive. I had earlier provided one to the Methodist Cottage staffers, but I also had my own copy. Jan, my friend that I met during my Alzheimer's journey, joined us at the hospital.

It was strangely quiet when we arrived. Most of the hospital staff were positioned at their posts, monitoring computer screens, doing paperwork, assembling medications, and going about their duties. I walked into Bert's room first. There were no tubes, no wires, no monitors with lights blinking signifying something to someone. Rather, it was soothingly silent, quietly comforting. I was by his side when Bert passed at 10:24 p.m. I touched his warm forehead and bid a farewell to my kind gentleman, my strong, loving, considerate, and loyal husband. The love of my life, a giant among men. Then I prayed:

"Thank you, God, for Bert's love and presence in my life. For better or for worse. It was you, Bert, who encouraged me to be me without doubt, without jealousy, without limits, without any negativity. You are now in a better place. God rest your soul."

The tears came again. I held his hand a moment longer, smoothed his receding blond hair toward his crown, kissed his lips, turned, and walked out of the room. At the door's threshold, I stopped and exhaled slowly and smoothly. I then released Bert.

"Good-bye, honey."

My family and I comforted each other and returned home. At midnight, we quietly welcomed in a new year.

~~~~~~~~

The week went by quickly. There were a million pieces to this puzzle that I had not yet completed. What to do first. I was on autopilot, doing what I had to do. Details, such as where to send the body, the cremation process, calls to be placed, service arrangements, musical selections, and gathering bits and pieces to be shared, needed my attention.

With Bert's passing, my grief turned to a slow, steady recall of all that he and I had been through over the past twenty-five years. Two heart attacks, prostrate cancer, two additional heart attacks and,
~~~~~~~~

finally, Alzheimer's in the last three years of his life. The good, the bad, the ugly. Through it all, I knew no one could take care of Bert better than I. I was committed and honored to do so until it was no longer possible. Even so, I felt relieved that he was no longer suffering from the slow, devastating ravages of this disease. No more suffering for Bert. No more suffering for me as well. Honestly, I was tired of being sad and worried and looked forward to the celebration of life service for my beloved Bert. Oh, that we could have had more time during our golden years.

~~~~~~~~

And so, here we are at Bert's one-hour celebration service. It's January 8, 2011. It is 2:00 p.m. We've been here for an hour already for the visitation time. This place is busy. There are signs before each mini chapel describing the person whose life is being recognized and celebrated. For us, the five-foot, 16×20 sign supported by a metal T bar displayed a cream-colored background with a color photo of Bert. It read, "Chapel A: Dr. Bert Hans Adams Saturday, 2:00 p.m. Chapel of Brooks-Wycliffe Visiting Hours Saturday, 1:00 p.m. until 2:00 p.m."
~~~~~~~~

The funeral director and his staff are professional looking and going about their business with an air of dignity, calmness, detachment, and curtness. They are used to this multiclient atmosphere where death becomes a profitable business. It is their goal to ensure the living have one last hurrah for their loved one.

According to his wishes, Bert was cremated within two days. His ashes were enclosed in a lovely urn. Inside the chapel, a six-foot wooden mahogany easel supported another 11×14 portrait, one of Bert's final official government pictures. He looks handsome: blond hair, piercing blue eyes, bushy brows, tanned complexion, that great smile showing his perfectly aligned orthodontist-aided teeth. A dark blue suit and tie hung from the broad shoulders of my rock, a dedicated public servant. The urn sits on a small table to the right of his photo. My mind shifts back to when we first met. What a daring and risky time for both of us, particularly me. Bert was and still is the kindest man I know. People from our work world, out-of-town colleagues, family, friends, and neighbors are here to bid farewell to this wonderful government employee. There's Joe Hinton from the DC district, Josh Watson from the LA district, Tony and Julie from the neighborhood association, friends

Jan and Sheba, and representatives from my loving church family.

While strains of Bert's various tastes in music fill the air – "Because You Love Me," "I Will Always Love You," "No Ordinary Love," "Dreams Come True," "You Were Always on My Mind," "Swing Low Sweet Chariot," and others by Sinatra, Stevie Wonder, Luther Vandross, Dionne Warrick, and Willie Nelson—I smile and offer conversation at every turn. At exactly 2:00 p.m., I am startled slightly by a shift from the meet and greet activity and exchanging niceties to the soft sweet sounds of the prelude, "Amazing Grace." People find their seats, quietly settled in, and turn to their program. The booklet is lovely and well done. Karen and my loving and attentive sisters did an exceptional job of putting together the four-page memorial for Bert. The embossed cream and gold tone program is neatly held together with a gold elastic rope string tied into a bow. "In Memory" is printed on the front cover. Inside is Bert's picture and life story.

"Be brief," Bert said during one of our conversations about his end-of-life journey.

Our assigned minister, a Chaplain Balman, offers a brief welcome, followed by a video capturing Bert's vibrant life. Each of us in the chapel is spellbound as we witness, laugh, comment, and reflect on what we see. The whole person, Bert, my man, his life unfolding before us: The fisherman, the homemaker, the builder, the public speaker, the teacher, the trainer, the family man, the corporate officer, the international diplomat, the proud and doting husband, the sibling, the cowboy, the animal lover, the golfer, the world traveler, the consummate and debonair dresser.

I take a deep breath and slowly and deliberately exhale. It is so moving; such wonderful memories flood my soul. I dab at my teary, swollen eyes as the video concludes. Chaplain Balman offers prayer and encouraging words of comfort. Again, I reflect on my wonderful life with Bert. It was a life I could not have had without him. I thought of growing up in Detroit, my marriage to Karen's father, divorcing him and moving to California, meeting Bert while married to Duke, and enjoying a wonderful working relationship that turned into some kind of other wonderful. Bert became my teacher, my mentor, my advisor, my confidant, my friend, my lover, my husband, and my all in all. Bert Adams was all that and a bag of chips.

Richard James, a musician from my church, soulfully renders "Jesus, You're the Center of My

Joy." Followed by a stirring message of condolence and ending with a final musical selection, "Stand," the grandchildren offer a right-on-time, lighthearted moment when they sang their version of "Bert's Song."

"O Lord, it's hard to be humble when I'm perfect in every way. Can't wait to look in the mirror, I get better lookin' each day. To know me is to love me, I must be a helluva man. O Lord, it's hard to be humble, but I'm doing the best I can." The weight in the room lifted. As I looked around the room, everyone is laughing cheerfully. My spirits are buoyed.

The concluding prayer is so very appropriate for Bert's life and ends with "I have fought the good fight, I have finished the race, I have kept the faith." (2 Timothy 4:7).

At 3:00 p.m. the service is complete. Your journey in this life is over. God rest your soul, Dr. Bert Hans Adams.

Lessons Learned:

> My relationship with Bert was a blessing.
> He brought out the best in me.

The caring nature of people amazes me. To the people who took time to support me in spite of their own issues, I am so very thankful.

Knowing that Bert is no longer in pain makes it easier to release him into God's hands.

I have no regrets for loving this man. I was his queen. He was my king.

Your Lessons:

____

____

____

____

CHAPTER 9

Grieving

"To live in the hearts of those we leave behind, is not to die."

This quote by Thomas Campbell, a Scottish poet, truly summarizes Bert's legacy. His home-going celebration was beautiful. Just as he wanted. Short, full of good, uplifting stories, stories of hope and of a life well lived.

The rest of the week was a blur. Of constant concern to me was the question "What would the rest of 2011 hold for me?" Though I was unsure, I was ready. "Bring it on!" was my mantra. At times, I felt shaky yet remarkably well. Recovery and stability for me is not yet real. I do know that I am tired of being tired. Tired of being sad and worried. But I know also that, with time, I will be better. Much better.

My immediate practical tasks kept me busy. There was, after all, the reality of managing the post funeral activities and the physical memories of Bert in our home. I became preoccupied with settlement of Bert's belongings. The children took items of clothing; others went to Goodwill. Still other items were relegated to a corner of his office, awaiting a time and place that was suitable for moving forward. I was not sleeping well. Most times, I was in our home alone.

Someone said to not make any important decisions when you are grieving. In February 2011, I asked my hairstylist to lighten my hair.

"Are you sure you want blond?"

"Yes!" I replied emphatically.

That was not an important decision. During the spring, Jan and I traveled to Charleston, South Carolina, and then abroad to Italy. Jan managed the myriad details. She loved it. We also traveled to Africa, including Kenya and Tanzania, then onto Venice, Greece, Paris, and Amsterdam. I was excited and loved the experience. Karen and I also did a weekend in Biloxi, Mississippi, enjoying the spa and gambling experience and savoring every minute of it.

Jan's husband, Lee, though worse, was still living in the long-term care facility at Clinton House. His passing in August 2011 was another blow to my sanity. Jan and I had been through so much together. Thank you, God, for your love and grace during Jan's distraughtness over the loss of Lee.

It was also in late 2011 that Sheba, another friend on this same mind-snatching journey, lost her husband, Larry. The three of us have been through so much together. I am thankful for their companionship. Who would have thought Alzheimer's would bring such diverse and different women together? A black woman, a white woman, and a Jewish woman. There's a blessing in everything we go through.

Shortly after Bert's passing, I became actively involved in arbitration work. Thank you, Bert, for encouraging me to learn a broader aspect of the business. Even though you are not with me physically, you are still taking care and watching over me. I am so very thankful. Little did I know that I wasn't quite ready to resume a full work schedule. Within months of Bert's passing, I packed a suitcase for an arbitration case in Borger, Texas, only to realize the night before that the case was scheduled at a later time. That was a signal that I was not doing as well as I thought. Jazzy and Billy Boy, my loving dogs, kept me company. Bert and I both enjoyed our animals. Yes, arbitration work is plentiful, and it can wait. Thank you, Bert, for encouraging me in that area, for plugging me into the good ole boys network, for willingly and unflinchingly sharing your "white privilege" status. You are and were a role model for how one's position in life can benefit others. Though you are no longer physically here, you are my guardian angel.

There are days when my mantra is "Bert, we had our time together. Now it is time for me to move on." Another mantra gets me through as well: "Though I am sad, it makes sense to feel this way." I am okay being sad and crying. I miss Bert tremendously, the old Bert, not the sick Bert. He was truly my rock. Everything he said or promised, he delivered. God bless you, my love. Often, I journal my thoughts to get some clarity. Watching TV, relaxing, and escaping are part of my days going forward. My family, including Karen and Faye, are always around. I love them dearly and am thankful that they are in my life. Yes, I am enjoying my alone time. I am not depressed or lonely. Yet I am excited to find my joy again.

~~~~~~~~
~~~~~~~~

I busy myself with nail appointments, pedicures, church activities, scripture readings, facials, massages, hair salon trips, exercise, lunch, wine tasting, and traveling abroad, and locally, golf, concerts, museum trips, dancing – lots of "me" time activities. I am happy. I love all of it. The focus is on me and stays on me. If that sounds selfish, then so be it. Ecclesiastes 3:1–4 reminds me that "to every thing there is a season, and a time to every purpose under the heaven: A time to be born, and a time to die; a time to plant, and a time to pluck up that which is planted; A time to kill, and a time to heal; a time to break down, and a time to build up; A time to weep, and a time to laugh; a time to mourn, and a time to dance." So today my mantra is "Let the dancing begin!" I took a salsa class and had a ball.

I tap into every resource to understand and manage my grief. Several books were helpful and reflective for me. One was Elizabeth Gilbert's *Eat, Pray, Love.* Somewhere in that book is the passage "I am the administrator of my own rescue." Those eight words strike a chord and stay with me. That's me. With good days and bad days, I am weary of suffering, weary of pain and of the loss. I felt like I needed some tools to totally heal and recover. I didn't want to just depend on time. And that is precisely why, six months after Bert's passing, I signed up and participated in a grief class. I needed to check myself! God sent me a sign. I was sitting in worship service and heard the announcement of a class called "Overcoming Loss Group Experience." I was curious. It met every other Wednesday for nine sessions and was scheduled to start in June 2011. The class description read "a group experience for those overcoming loss in their lives." I was interested and intrigued. I thought I was okay. I mean, some days were better than others, but overall I thought I was okay, all right. I mentioned the grief class to my good friends and neighbors.

"You're doing just fine, Ramel. You don't need that class."

"Why drudge up the past? Move forward."

What a prince of a man Bert was. I have loved him so much. I signed up for the June class. I am glad I did. Ultimately, this class was extremely helpful and benefited me in more ways than I imagined. The sessions opened me up to all of me, parts of me that I hadn't consciously considered: my hormone levels, my energy level, heightened awareness of what's going on in my body. There were twenty willing participants who were or had experienced various losses – including divorce, battling diseases, missing a child, pet deaths. They too were suffering through some of life's most stressful events.

A highlight of my class was to write your loved one a letter as if you were literally speaking to him. And so, on July 17, 2011, seven months after Bert's passing, I penned this letter to my beloved:

Dear Bert:

I have written so much of my thoughts and experiences since your passing in my journal. In fact, I started to write in the journal while you were at Methodist Cottage. I was feeling so overwhelmed, sad, and helpless during that time. It had been so long since I felt the normal man that I've loved and cherished. Of course, I still loved you, but missed our "normal" relationship. You were my best friend, teacher, nourisher, confidant, husband and, once upon a time, lover. I now reflect back on our lives only to realize through your heart attacks, cancer, and lastly, Alzheimer's, we had not been sexual. However, the intimacy and love remained. Even now.

At the present time, reflections of how our relationship and marriage have been clear. I have time to think. You have given me much. Also, you have required much care. However, I have no regrets. Only the loving memories sustain the emptiness. I must feel some anger over how much it has taken of my life to care for your continual declining health. Bert, I really attribute this anger to the loss of you through the Alzheimer's desease . . . disease (see, I cannot even spell as well anymore).

In addition, because of so much illness during our marriage, I do not think I will remarry even when I become ready to date. For one, I do not want the responsibility of taking care of another spouse. Secondly, I do not feel someone would be a good husband as you have been throughout the years. Seriously, your kindness, goodness, generosity, and super intelligence are huge attributes for someone to overcome. First, it took years in the beginning to develop friendship, respect, and trust. I really do not have time (age) and energy to go through the process again. Plus, I do not want to be hurt. I don't want to compromise too much again. I do realize I will probably have a male friend eventually. Maybe sex too (smile)!

But what I do know is God has a plan for me. I must remain healthy in spirit and body. And I must say good-bye to you, my love, for it is time to move on.

Love,
R

Nearly a year after Bert's passing, on November 1, 2011, my oldest grandson, Chip, and I released his ashes at the Winter Hill's Golf Course, a place Bert and I often frequented. I also read Steve Harvey's book *Straight Talk, No Chaser* to reconnect my sensual and sexual side. You see, I anticipate new relationships and new journeys. I long for renewed passion and male friendships.

Sadly, Sheba committed suicide within two years of Larry's death. Though she had two children, grandchildren, and other family members in the Philadelphia area, Sheba mourned and missed her husband terribly and had great difficulty moving on. Jan has moved on with her life and is happily dating.

Finally, Billy Boy, one of my dogs who brought joy to the Alzheimer's patients, died the following spring of 2012. In the midst of life, death exists. That's the way life is.

Lessons Learned:

> If you think you're okay, perhaps you're really not. After all is said and done, after you've listened to your loved ones and others, after you've settled into a night of sleeplessness, of tossing and turning, do what you think is best for you.
>
> Friendships, like love, come in all shades and colors. Leave yourself open to these wonders of life.
>
> God is good and he has a plan and a purpose for our lives. We need to stop, think, pray, and hear him.
>
> Hold on to your faith, whatever it is. There is a higher power, so when you come to the end of your rope, tie a knot in it and look to the hills. Find your hope.

Live your life to the fullest. If there is something you want to do, do it.

There are tools to assist you in your loss journey; whatever they are, use them. Don't be afraid to take a class on grieving or see a psychologist. My "Overcoming Loss" class at church was magnificent. My goal was to be confident of the progress experienced through the healing process.

From your valley experience, prepare to become whole again; do not allow a loss to burden a new relationship.

I want my life to have made a difference in someone else's life. That is the purpose of this book.

Bert would be pleased with this book! And with my hair!

Your Lessons:

CHAPTER 10

Love in My Winter Season

It's been over three year since Bert's passing. I still cannot say "death." My life as I knew it will never be the same. I am still handling details related to his life, our life, together. Work, I must say, is a sweet relief remedy. My extensive experience as a neutral mediation arbitrator representing clients in all types of forums, in various sectors, serves me well. My network is active. Industry clients request my service. Work is plentiful. I can do it without frustration. Thank God! And thank you, Bert, for encouraging me and for being my angel. You said I'd have plenty of work. As usual, you are still a man of your word even though you are no longer here.

My love life, relationship wise, is still in need of repair. Though I've been a widow for three years, it's really been eight years since I've had intimacy, real intimacy. Bert and I were great teammates and the best of friends; we were soul mates. There was, however, no sex, no intimacy, during our last eight years together because of his illnesses.

Which brings me to a New Year's resolution I made in January 2013: to start dating. Paying more attention to my "me" time, which includes plenty of socializing, I planned a trip to the West Coast to visit friends there. I hadn't seen many of them for some time, perhaps a year or two, and wanted to get caught up. A golf tournament seemed a good reason to make the trip. Bert taught me the game of golf. He and I played many rounds for business, pleasure, and network building. My golf clubs were in need of swinging. I literally had to dig them out of the garage and dust each iron, club by club. It had been at least three or four months since I even touched a golf club.

Whenever I made plans to play, something came up. I am forever working my contractor arbitration business. There are always arbitration cases to review, write and forward, as I am on a preferred list of contractors called upon regularly for work across the USA. My usual schedule is get a call, review the details, receive the pertinent documents, accept the assignment, travel to the face-to-face meeting, conduct the hearing, make a decision, write the case, mail the decision via overnight delivery, send an invoice, and get my money!

I rarely allowed myself the opportunity to think about romance again; sex was out of reach. Just having a male friend was a remote thought. Like when Karen and I first moved to California to pursue my career dreams thirty years ago, I was never closed about having men in my life. It was just not front and center in my thoughts.

I have, though, often thought of what my next mate, companion, man, would look like. Will he be African American? Would I fall in love again with a Caucasian? Does it really matter? What's it like to kiss and hold someone again? It seems I haven't had sex in a lifetime. I miss intimacy and fun and being in love. I am petrified of dating or having another mate. I do know I have room in my heart for passion and friendship with another person at some point. I briefly joined a relationship dating service. Not for me!

On this lovely hot, arid day, here I am in Mesa, Arizona, at River Oaks Golf Club, an exclusive enclave of well-manicured greens, sprawling homes with winding driveways, fine luxury cars, boats, and golfers young and old, enjoying myself. I am surrounded by friends and their friends, having a great time. Moving through the day was easy. I always enjoy being outdoors. Though I didn't play very well, the exercise, being close to nature, reconnecting, and making new friends made the event and the trip more than worthwhile. I had fun!

Dinner afterward was in the formal dining area of the clubhouse. As I was one of the first to finish my round, I passed through the food line rather quickly. The menu included baked chicken, baked beans, coleslaw, rolls, bottled water (or soda; I chose the water) and, for dessert, something decadent: A chocolate-frosted brownie with chocolate chips inside. I was set to sit down and grub a little. I took several bites of the moist chicken; it was delicious. Baked just right, not tough, with some sort of citrus, honey glaze sauce covering it. Worth dipping my roll into the sweet, tangy juice.

My eyes perused the large dining hall, taking in the sights and sounds of a just finished golf tournament.

People were coming and going. There were lots of laughter and jovial conversation in the room. I was just about to sip my drink when I spotted a fine specimen of a man seemingly looking for a place to sit his food down and eat. Our eyes connected, his deep-set brown eyes with a glint of mischief in them staring at me. He was tall, milk-chocolate-candy-bar dark, and handsome! I motioned him to my table. He smiled as he approached the empty seat on my right.

"Hi, I'm Ramel."

"Hello," he chimed in, "how was your round?"

"It was great. I'm famished! This meal is just right!"

He sat his plate down next to mine, returned to get his soda, pulled his chair out and sat down – those mischievous eyes still taking me in. Without hesitation, he said, "I'm Mark. Good to meet ya!"

And so began love in the winter season of my life. It's been over a year since this beautiful African American man sat at my dinner table. Mark's a widower, been one for two years. When we met, he was six months into his journey without his soul mate. He's the same age as I. That's a switch. Remember my daddy issues? We have many things in common. He has moved from the West Coast to Florida (closer to me) and started a new life. I am part of it. Passion has returned; it's different. It's great! Lovemaking is in my future. I am happy. My joy is back. I am blessed to be in this place. This story is not over. Stay tuned.

Lessons Learned:

> The lesson is that lessons still come. They are lifelong.
>
> Take good care of yourself. Take all the time you need to heal.
>
> *Mashed Potatoes in My Salad* is a metaphor for life. Though they may be different, things may not be that bad. Get over it, and keep it moving.
>
> Tune in to your spiritual self and nurture yourself.
>
> Be open to love anywhere, anytime, and with anyone.

Connect with whomever you are supposed to connect with. For me, my basic parameters are, he needs to be "a man's man" What is that, you ask? Someone not into building egos. He must be young in spirit, not too old (not sure yet what "too old" is), active, and fun loving.

Claim your story and tell it! What are you waiting for?

There is always a new chapter in life. You never know what it is. God has a plan for you. Do the work on yourself and prepare to receive the blessing.

Having gone through my valleys of illness after illness, caregiving is part of who I am. However, I sure do appreciate Mark, and it's time to reclaim my joy.

My story is still being written. It is constantly evolving – with that milk chocolate man. Bert would be pleased.

Your Lessons:

Order Form

Thank you for purchasing *Mashed Potatoes in My Salad.*

Log on to our website at: www.eunicelsykes.com to share your comments or mail to:

Eunice L Sykes
PO Box 2651
McDonough, GA 30253

eunsyk06@myway.com

I would love to hear from you.

To purchase limited editions of two of my books listed below, please specify the book you are ordering and send check or money order to address above.

From Kibler's Bridge to Miller Road: 65 Years of Christian Service in the African Methodist Episcopal Church. $10.00 + $3.00 S&H (hardback with dustcover)

Instant Church: My Millennium Musings (selected poems). $2.00 + $1.00 S&H (paperback)

Order both books for $15 (including S&H)

CPSIA information can be obtained at www.ICGtesting.com
Printed in the USA
LVOW11*0224301014
411142LV00002B/2/P

9 781499 061680